SUPER SPINACH

Also by Hannah Shaw

KITTEN LADY'S BIG BOOK OF LITTLE KITTENS

Adventures in Fosterland series
EMMETT AND JEZ

KITTEN LADY

HANNAH SHAW

Adventures in
FOSTERLAND

Illustrated by
BEV JOHNSON

SUPER SPINACH

Aladdin
New York London Toronto Sydney New Delhi

ALADDIN

An imprint of Simon & Schuster Children's Publishing Division

1230 Avenue of the Americas, New York, New York 10020

First Aladdin paperback edition June 2022

Copyright © 2022 by Kitten Lady, LLC

Also available in an Aladdin hardcover edition.

All rights reserved, including the right of reproduction in whole or in part in any form.

ALADDIN and related logo are registered trademarks of Simon & Schuster, Inc.

For information about special discounts for bulk purchases, please contact Simon & Schuster Special Sales at 1-866-506-1949 or business@simonandschuster.com.

The Simon & Schuster Speakers Bureau can bring authors to your live event. For more information or to book an event contact the Simon & Schuster Speakers Bureau at 1-866-248-3049 or visit our website at www.simonspeakers.com.

Designed by Tiara Iandiorio

The illustrations for this book were rendered digitally.

The text of this book was set in Banda.

Manufactured in the United States of America 0422 OFF

2 4 6 8 10 9 7 5 3 1

Library of Congress Cataloging-in-Publication Data

Names: Shaw, Hannah René, 1987- author. | Johnson, Beverly, illustrator.

Title: Super Spinach / by Hannah Shaw ; illustrated by Bev Johnson.

Description: First Aladdin paperback edition. | New York : Aladdin, 2022. | Series: Adventures in Fosterland | Summary: After undergoing a procedure at the vet, a kitten takes on the persona of Super Spinach and goes to Fosterland, where she and her sidekick Chickpea help a litter of kittens.

Identifiers: LCCN 2021047699 (print) | LCCN 2021047700 (ebook) | ISBN 9781665901253 (hc) | ISBN 9781665901246 (pbk) | ISBN 9781665901260 (ebook)

Subjects: CYAC: Cats—Fiction. | Animals—Infancy—Fiction. | Foster care of animals—Fiction.

Classification: LCC PZ7.1.S4935 Su 2022 (print) | LCC PZ7.1.S4935 (ebook) | DDC [Fic]—dc23

LC record available at https://lccn.loc.gov/2021047699

LC ebook record available at https://lccn.loc.gov/2021047700

To every kid and kitten
searching for their inner power

Contents

CHAPTER 1

The White Card

"Pow!" shouted a tiny tabby named Bruce as his paw struck a crinkle ball, sending it flying toward his litter-mates.

"Bam!" called his sister, Sally, as she swiped it out of the air with her fluffy mitts.

Slam! Two calicos named Prissy and Peach jumped for the ball and collided.

The four kittens were tucked into the

back room of an animal shelter, tumbling in their metal kennel like furry wrestlers. Across the way, they had an audience of one: a tiny little kitten named Spinach who was peering at them through the bars of her own separate kennel.

Although Spinach longed to play with the shiny toy that had captured the other kittens' attention, she couldn't join in on the fun. Instead, she sat with her face smooshed against the metal poles, taking shallow breaths and watching as the ball bounced from paw to paw, imagining how fun it would be to play, too. But she was smaller and frailer than the other kittens, and in no condition to be twisting, jumping, rolling, or sprinting. And so there she sat, stuck on the sidelines while the others perfected their pounces.

"Think fast!" called Sally as she threw the crinkle ball straight into the air. Prissy, Peach, and Bruce all made a leap for it, colliding on top of the ball and falling into a pile of laughter.

"Hey, keep it down up there!" grumbled Jack, the cat in the kennel below them. "I'm trying to get some beauty rest before my big adoption day."

The kittens rolled their eyes and kept playing. They had so much energy!

Bam! Bam! Pow! The ball flew back and forth across the kennel.

Sally slammed against the bars as she

swiped the ball into the kennel corner, where Spinach could get a closer look at the glittery toy. Spinach giggled as she watched. "That looks fun! I wish I could play."

"Sorry, Spinach! It's just . . . you know," Sally said with a shrug. She picked up the ball in her mouth and trotted back over to her siblings.

"I know," Spinach said to no one, and shrank into the corner of the cage.

The trouble is, Spinach *didn't* know. Well, she *sort of* knew that she was different, but she didn't really know *why*. All she knew was that her whole life, she'd been unable to do the things that other kittens her age could do. She

was easily winded—even walking to the water dish caused her to wheeze—so playtime was not an option. That was just the way it was.

Spinach had silver fur with gray tiger stripes, but she didn't feel like a tiger at all. Tigers run and pounce and go on adventures, but Spinach couldn't do any of those things. She had been born with an extra-small, misshapen rib cage that made it difficult for her to breathe deeply or walk comfortably. Anytime her chest was touched, it sent a prickly feeling through her body, like her heart was caught in a cactus garden. Because of this, she had always been a very cautious kitten who moved slowly, kept to herself, and didn't take many risks.

Of course, Spinach didn't know life any other way, and she was quite used to passing the days sitting very still, quietly observing the world around her through soft almond-shaped eyes. But deep inside, she longed for the friendship and adventure all the other kittens seemed to have.

Sigh. Alone in her kennel, Spinach had nothing but a litter box, a water dish, and a front-row seat to watch the other kittens playing without her.

Spinach hung her head and looked down at her paws. The newspaper that lined her kennel was making her daydream about the world beyond the bars. In the printed pictures, everyone seemed to have a friend: the business-people, the models, and even the *cartoon characters*! She squinted at a superhero comic showing a crime-fighting duo flying through the sky. It seemed like they had it all: amazing costumes, cool gadgets, and an entire cast of supporting characters. It didn't make sense that her life had to be so boring . . . and so lonely. Why did everyone else get to have all the fun? Spinach closed her eyes and imag-ined soaring through the air and doing important things like saving babies and protecting the world from bad guys.

But then the image faded, and she sighed. Spinach knew she could never do any of that.

When Spinach looked up, Bruce, Sally, Prissy, and Peach had lost interest in the crinkle ball, and now they all sat admiring the blue card that hung on their kennel. The card was just placed there today, and it was a big event in the life of any shelter cat. Probably the most important of all!

"You know, once you get a blue card clipped to your kennel, it means you're about to go out to the adoption floor! I heard it from Wilson, the black cat who used to live in cage six. Once his blue card arrived, it was only a matter of hours before he found his home!" Bruce said, tapping at the card. "This thing is a one-way ticket to Foreverland!"

"No more cages, just a big house and a family to call your own . . . ," said Peach. "Prissy, we'll go to a home together, right? Priss?"

Prissy smiled and nodded her head. "Sisters stick together for life!"

Sally bumped her shoulders with Bruce and announced, "Every kitten needs a sidekick!"

Spinach looked at them longingly, then looked back at her lonely cage. *If every kitten needs a sidekick, then where is mine?* All her life she'd been the outcast—too petite to play with the others, too fragile to find a friend. Everyone had a buddy but her.

Well, there *was* one other cat who was alone—Jack. Spinach tilted her head as she looked down at him, all curled up on a donut bed in the kennel below, sleeping the day away. "Excuse me, I'm sorry to pester you, but . . . are you . . . would you happen to . . . might you be looking for a sidekick?" Spinach crossed her toe beans, hoping.

Jack yawned and looked up at her. "Eh, that's real sweet, kid, but I'm kind of a loner. Besides, I'm getting adopted today, remember?" He pressed his nose against the kennel, and his blue card glimmered.

"Oh," Spinach said. "Well, that's okay.

Congratulations on your big day. . . ."

She slumped over in the corner of her cage. Where was *her* blue card?

Spinach tapped against the bar and quietly asked the kittens, "Do you think I'll ever get a blue card, too?"

"I'm sure yours is coming any minute," Sally said, holding up a comforting paw. She opened her mouth to say more, but then—

Click! A shelter worker had returned, and she had clipped a card onto Spinach's cage. For a moment, Spinach felt a flutter of excitement, but the feeling vanished when she saw that the card looked different from the others. It wasn't blue—it was white.

Why does my card look different? Spinach wondered. *What does this mean?* With small, shallow breaths, she could feel her chest getting tighter as panic set in. "Does anyone know why my card is white?"

Peach looked to Prissy. Prissy looked to Bruce. Bruce looked to Sally. And Sally just scratched her head, confused.

But Jack, the big cat in the kennel below, spoke up. "Yeah, I know that card, kid. A white card means a visit with the white-coat people. I think they're called a vetrin . . . a vetrinaire . . . Well, I don't know how to pronounce it. They're basically called a vet or something. They are the ones who show up when a cat needs help. That's *you*, kid."

Spinach's heart was thump-thump-thumping in her tiny chest, which was ever so uncomfortable. She knew that the white-coat people, who were apparently called *vets*, were there to help, but she didn't like the sound of visiting them at all. She wanted to go to the adoption floor!

Just then, a shelter employee in a blue shirt came and picked up Jack. As he exited the room in her arms, he turned to Spinach and said, "The road to Foreverland is ever-winding, kid. It ain't the same for every cat. I mean, look at me! I'm just now finding my forever home, and I'm fifteen years old. Imagine that—a hefty old guy like me! Don't worry 'bout it, kid. Your time will come—!" The door closed and he was gone.

Spinach looked to the others with distress. "Is everyone really getting adopted but me?"

"Oh, Spinach, it's okay," Sally said. "It's like the old guy said. You just have a different pathway . . . a special journey you have to take. That's all."

"But I don't want a different pathway," Spinach wheezed, reaching through the bars to try to bat the card away and make it all stop. "I want to be adopted with you guys!"

Spinach tried and tried, but she couldn't take the card down.

"Turn blue!" she called out as she bopped the card, hoping for it to magically transform. But she had no power in her paws, and in all her smacking, she had only succeeded in making it swing back and forth, taunting her as it moved side to side, undeniably *white*.

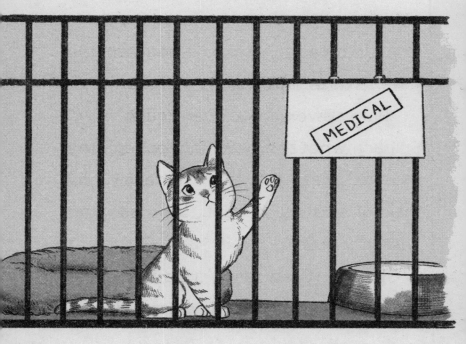

The door opened again, and two workers in blue shirts approached the kennel, which rattled as it unlocked. The other kittens were being plucked from the cage faster than Spinach could catch her breath to say goodbye. Peach, Prissy, Sally, and Bruce were whisked away to the adoption floor—and all Spinach could do was take tiny breaths and watch as they left her behind.

"We believe in you!" said Peach.

"You've got this, Spinach. You're going to make it to Foreverland someday. All you have to do is follow the path and *believe in yourself!*" said Sally.

Spinach pressed her little pink nose between the bars, very much in *dis*belief.

The kittens were gone, and she was left with nothing but a white card and tears in her eyes.

Believe in myself? Spinach thought. *What's there to believe in?*

CHAPTER 2

Your Heart Is in Danger

Within minutes, the white coats had come and taken Spinach to a large and echoey room where she was surrounded by staring eyes. The cold metal table felt like ice cubes against her paw pads, which was *almost* enough to distract her from her confusion and frustration, and the strange sensation of hands reaching out to touch her.

"Excuse me, but I think there's been some kind of mistake," she said to a white-coat lady. "I think I'm supposed to have received my blue card. . . . Ouch!" She jolted back as fingers wiggled over her rib cage. "Hey, that hurts!"

The white-coat lady wasn't listening, or maybe she didn't understand. And so Spinach scanned the room sideways, looking outward in hope of finding answers.

She listed in her head all the things she could see.

A glass container filled with little snowballs.

Another filled with small sticks.

A tray with some shiny things on it.

A strange robot machine . . . or some-thing like that.

It calmed her down, but she was still in the pickle of not knowing where she was, or why she couldn't go to Foreverland.

On the far side of the room, she spotted a small row of cages. A big yellow dog with a cone on his head was resting on the lower level. On the upper level, an orange cat was napping with his leg wrapped in a purple cast. The third cage was empty. Was it for her?

She called out to the dog and cat. "Hello? I'm sorry to wake you, but I was supposed to receive a blue card, and I received a white card instead. I think it might be a mix-up, but if not . . . could you please tell me what exactly happens in here?" The dog with the cone and the cat with the cast continued their naps and didn't respond.

Then a hand scooped Spinach up and carried her over to the robot machine. *Agh!* She closed her eyes, wincing as she was placed at the center of its crosshairs. She took a few shallow breaths and opened her eyes but was immediately startled again by a sudden flash of lightning, which made a loud *click!* that caused everyone to jump— her, the dog, and the orange cat, both of whom didn't look very happy about being woken up.

Spinach was feeling confused. "A dif-

ferent pathway," she whispered to herself. *What could that mean?*

Then, from the corner of her eye, she
noticed a scraggly old tomcat stretching
out his legs from behind a stack of files.

Having just taken his afternoon snooze,
the cat stood up and sauntered along the
counter. He had puffy cheeks, a raggedy
folded ear, wiry whiskers that stuck out
in every direction, and most importantly,
he had free rein of the room.

Spinach perked up. She called out to
him: "Excuse me, Mr. Tomcat? Do you
know what's going on here?"

The cat approached her and sat
down, observing her quizzically and
twirling his crinkly eyebrow whiskers

with his paw. "That's *Dr.* Tomcat, if you don't mind. Welcome to the clinic, young one. What ails you?"

"Oh, um, thank you . . . *Dr.* Tomcat. Anyway, I seem to have received a white card, but I was meant to receive one in blue." If Spinach just kept repeating this, maybe she could make it true.

"Ah, yes, my dear! All the kittens who come through here have received a white card, of course. That's your ticket to the veterinarian, after all! Yes, I've seen many a sickly cat come through these doors . . . many a broken leg . . . many an oozing wound. . . ."

Spinach's face scrunched up. "Well, I'm not broken! Or . . . oozing!"

"Yes, yes. Well, let's see. I'm sure I can determine precisely why you are here with a quick look at your chart." He paused for a yawn, then looked up at a screen behind him and squinted. On the screen, there was a black-and-white image of kitten bones.

"Pectus excavatum," he said.

Spinach tilted her head. "Huh?"

"Pectus excavatum," he repeated, pointing to the image.

She blinked, confused. "Is that some kind of . . . magic spell? Are you a wizard?"

He shook his head. "I wish I was, because you could certainly use a little magic! No, no, I'm just a clinic cat, well studied after years of living here in the veterinary office. I've been around a long time, and I dare say that's the worst case of pectus excavatum I've *ever* seen." He looked back at the screen. "Just look at your chest: so small and so compressed. Your heart is in danger, my dear!"

Spinach looked at the screen, not knowing how to take in what she was seeing and hearing. Was that image really of her? It didn't have fur or whiskers, but it was certainly shaped like a little cat.

At the center of the image, a heart was trapped within small, pointy, misshapen bones, and it hit her: she really was different from the others. And that was why she couldn't go to Foreverland.

With a lump in her throat, she whispered, "What's going to happen to me?"

"The vets will do their best to fix you up like those two." He gestured to the

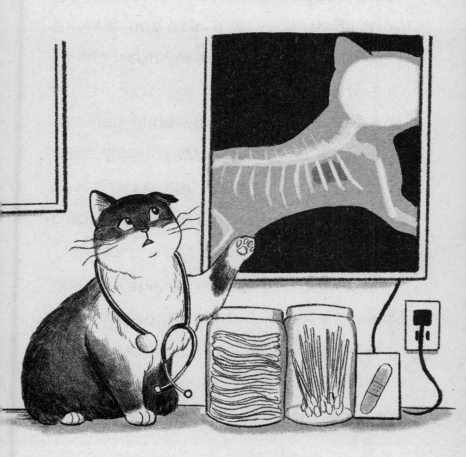

dog in the cone and the cat with the wrapped leg. "They'll perform a special surgery, under my supervision, of course, and bandage you up with armor on your chest. After that, if you're lucky, you'll go off to Fosterland for recovery," said Dr. Tomcat.

Fosterland, Spinach noted to herself.

"But I'll be honest with you, my dear: it's all a big *if.* Because *that* doesn't look good." He pointed to the X-ray. "You'd have to have superpowers to survive that."

This Dr. Tomcat was *not* helping Spinach's fears! Before she could process what he had just said, or respond, a white-coat lady swooped her up and took her into an operating room filled with bright lights and beeping machines.

With every thump of her heart, Spinach could feel her chest getting tighter, and she couldn't stop thinking about what the old tomcat had said about the danger she was in.

And she trembled at the realization that she did not have superpowers at all.

Oh, if only she *did* have superpowers! She would fly right off the table and whoosh through the window to escape! Of course, she didn't dare to try, as all her life she could barely even walk comfortably. So instead she covered her eyes, simply wishing she had the power to teleport far, far away. But when she peeked through her paws, she was still on the operating table . . . and a sharp needle was pointed right at her! She closed her eyes tightly, longing for the power to make herself completely invisible.

A mask went over her face, and the world slowly disappeared.

For a long while, she felt nothing.

She heard nothing.

She saw nothing.

But eventually, she heard a faint sound in the distance and began to slowly wake.

Beep. Beep. Beep.

Spinach squinted her eyes open, but everything was hazy. She tried to stand up—and fell right down! *Whoa.* She gazed down at her blurry paws and felt the room spin.

Had her invisibility trick worked? Her head bobbled as she tried her best to steady herself with wobbly front legs. But what was this? A long white vine was attached to her leg with a bandage. She followed the vine with her eyes and saw that it ran up and out of the cage where she was now resting.

Spinach took a deep breath and paused. *Hmm.* She took another deep breath. And another. Confused, Spinach inhaled slowly and deeply, holding her breath for a moment, then exhaling. *Wait a minute,* she thought to herself. *Since when can I take a deep breath?*

She held her paw to her chest and felt
that she was now wearing a hard shield
where there used to just be fur.

What's this?

Fighting to keep her eyes open and
focused, she squinted at the wall of the
cage. In the silver reflection, she saw a
new kitten: a little gray tiger cat with

built-in armor on her chest. She gasped! And for once in her life, gasping didn't hurt.

From between the bars, she spun her dizzy head and saw that Dr. Tomcat was looking back at her in amazement. As she stood before him in her brand-new chest armor, he gave her a wink and a snaggletoothed grin. "Good for you, my dear! You're a survivor. Guess you must be some kind of superhero after all!"

CHAPTER 3

Super-Kitten
Incoming

Despite her excitement over this new sensation of breathing deeply, Spinach was exhausted from her long day and had drifted off to sleep. When she woke up, she suddenly found herself ascending like a balloon filled with air. Up, up, and away!

"Whoa!" she called out, steadying herself against the blanket beneath her paws.

She stood at attention, hovering two

feet from the ground in some sort of flying contraption. This strange floating vessel was similar to the cage she had been in at the vet clinic, but it was smaller and with little windows from which she could see that she was traveling through a neighborhood.

What is this thing? Am I flying?

Here she was, dressed in some sort of armor, feeling stronger than ever— and now she was *floating through the air?* Dr. Tomcat had said she must be a superhero. Could it be true?

Maybe this is some kind of . . . super-vehicle? She zoomed through the streets, levitating over the sidewalk. "Look out!" she called out as a person carrying

groceries walked toward her. Spinach zipped to the left, just narrowly dodging a long baguette jutting out from a paper sack.

Can this really be? My very own cat-mobile?!

She looked straight ahead and saw a child on a bicycle clumsily headed her way. "Super-kitten incoming!" she yelled. Spinach leaned to the right, and her super-vehicle moved with her— just in time to avoid slamming into the handlebars.

Just as soon as she felt she was getting the hang of steering her cat-mobile, Spinach peered into the distance and saw that dozens of cars were speeding across the road ahead. Above them, a big red light was pointing in her direction. She was hurling toward the edge of the sidewalk and bracing for impact.

"Code red! How do I stop this thing?!"

She looked all over for some kind of button or lever to make the cat-mobile stop. But there was nothing that could help her! Out of options, she yelled, "STOP!" and the vehicle slowed to a pause.

Dang, it's got a voice-operated control system? That's fancy.

As she launched her hovercraft farther into the neighborhood, she couldn't help but smile at how incredible it all was. Just days ago, she was sitting sadly in the corner of a cage at the animal shelter, hardly able to breathe, and now she was inhaling fresh summer air—and it seemed that she might be an *actual superhero* at the helm of her own cat-mobile! If only the shelter kittens could see her now! It was clear that she was a sight to behold, because no one could take their eyes off her. The humans stared in awe, the dogs yapped with jealousy, and she even passed a little pink pig who was tilting his head in amazement!

"Cat-mobile, take me to Fosterland!" she commanded, remembering the tom- cat's words, and, turning away from the sidewalk, she floated toward a house.

The door opened magically—like this was exactly where she belonged. As her cat-mobile landed in the hallway, she looked around her new headquarters, took a deep breath, and smiled.

Things seemed to be looking up for

Spinach! Now that she had found her way to Fosterland, she was escorted to her very own kitten fortress: an impressive suite with a large bathroom, a big bed to sleep in, and various training stations, all secured within tall translucent walls.

This must be my super-station, she thought.

Non-Super Spinach would have huddled in a corner, taking it easy and trying not to get out of breath. But not anymore! For the first time in her life, Spinach was feeling little spurts of confidence. Her mind felt sharp, and her body felt more comfortable than ever before—that is, aside from having this thing on her chest!

She touched her chest plate, which was hard and shiny. *Heroes need armor,* she told herself, but she wasn't sure how exactly she was going to walk while wearing something so clunky. She lifted her paw up and over the plate and pushed it forward in an attempt to take a step, but quickly fell to her side. *Oof!* She shook her head and tried again. *Lift, push, step. Lift, push, step.*

In this clumsy manner, she high-stepped around the perimeter of her super-station. As she stomped along, she passed several large pieces of training equipment, including a crinkly tunnel, a tether ball, and a rope pole that was ten times her height! Her tummy filled with butterflies as she laid her eyes on all the things she would soon learn to do.

Just as she was thinking it was time for a snack, in walked a giant lady holding a dish of fishy food.

Spinach looked at her quizzically. *A whole dish of fishies just for me? Could this be my superhero helper . . . like the heroes in the comic strip had?*

"You must be . . . my purrsonal assistant!" Spinach exclaimed.

Spinach munched with determination. *Superheroes need to eat extra!* She ate until she was filled to the brim, her tiny tummy puffing out like she'd swallowed a small water balloon. With great fervor, she tried to lick away the little gravy mustache that had formed around her mouth. Spinach paused mid-blep to ponder what other accommodations were in store now that she was in her super-station. *I wonder if there are any moist towelettes. . . .*

Tap-tap-tap. The lady cleaned her face with a warm wet cloth.

Spinach gasped. *How did she know? This place is almost too good to be true!*

From what Spinach could tell so far, her new purrsonal assistant seemed to know exactly what she needed, which was very peculiar because she wasn't used to humans being able to understand her. *Could this be one of my superpowers? I have the power to . . . communicate with humans?* She gave it a shot.

"Excuse me, can I ask you a question?" Spinach meowed, but the assistant didn't respond.

"EXCUSE MEEE-OOOW!"

The assistant picked up Spinach and lifted her high until they were face-to-face. The way she gazed upon her, so curious and inquisitive, it seemed she could almost see through Spinach's eyes all the way into her brain. And so Spinach, deciding telepathy must be the key to her human-communication superpower, tried to send her a message with her mind:

Dear purrsonal assistant, if you can hear me, give me a sign.

The purrsonal assistant kissed her on the nose. Spinach's eyes grew wide—this was certainly a sign that she could communicate with humans using only her mind! She continued:

Purrsonal assistant, I've only just begun to understand the strange powers I possess and this mission that I must go on. If this is truly the path that I am meant to take, please show me . . . what more must I do to complete my superhero transformation?

With a gentle pet on the head, the assistant lowered her back into her

fortress and walked over to a large set of drawers, which she opened. She pulled out a peculiar piece of fabric the size and shape of a foot and held it up to Spinach's chest.

What does this mean?

Snip-snip-snip. She began to cut away at the fabric, shortening it and adding two small holes on the side. A few times she held it up to the light, paused, then cut away at it some more. The floor was now covered with tiny scraps, and the assistant was holding a small outfit custom-cut from a cloth sock.

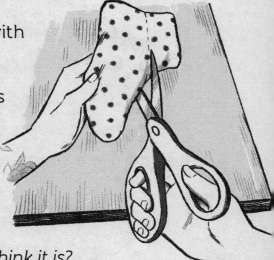

Is this what I think it is?

She slowly lowered the fabric over Spinach's head, gently placing it over the chest armor. She carefully pulled her paws through the perfectly placed openings and tugged at the bottom until the outfit was fitted over her torso.

Spinach stood taller than ever before, basking in the glorious feeling that her powers were starting to grow. She lifted one paw to the air and cried out with joy:

"My transformation is officially complete: I've got a *super-sock!*"

CHAPTER 4

I Can Fly

It was undeniable: Spinach was a super-hero, and now she truly looked the part. The polka-dot cotton sock was perfectly tailored, holding her chest armor firmly in place with a flattering fit. Her front legs had never looked so muscular and capable as they did now that she was wearing a sleeveless top. And best of all, her chest armor felt much more comfortable and snug in the protection of the sock. She strutted with ease, emboldened by her powerful new super-suit.

From the corner of her eye, she noticed that a white cat was staring at her from across the way. She had one eye, which was gazing at Spinach with curiosity. *Could this be another super-hero?* she wondered.

The white cat approached the clear glass pen, tilting her head to the side. "Are you wearing a sock?"

Feeling quite brave, Spinach puffed out her chest armor and introduced her-self. "It's my super-suit! And I'm Super Spinach, at your service."

The white cat smirked, looking her up and down with her yellow eye. "Oh, a super-suit. Of course it is. How silly of me."

"Am I to understand that this is some sort of hero training academy? Are you the headmistress?" *Or,* Spinach worried, *could she be a villain?* Spinach hoped for headmistress—she wasn't ready to take down any bad guys just yet.

Eloise smiled. "The headmistress? Yes, I like that. . . . That's got a nice ring to it. I'm Eloise. Ahem—*Headmistress* Eloise."

Spinach sighed with relief. "Fantastic! Listen, I'm not sure what's going on here, but ever since I woke up with this *thing* on my chest, everything has changed. I keep discovering these strange powers I never had before. Like earlier today, I *flew a cat-mobile*. Can you believe it? Then I sent a telepathic message to a human. If I'm here for a mission, please . . . tell me everything I need to know."

Eloise paused to think before speaking in rhyme:

**"You are special, I can see,
so have no doubt or fear.
Remember, strength and
bravery
come only from right here."**

Eloise pointed to Spinach's chest. Spinach sighed. "Yeah, I know, my

strength comes from my chest armor." She tapped at her chest piece with a *thunk-thunk-thunk*. "You've got that much right. Anything else?"

Eloise patted her on the head. "You're cute. Stay out of trouble." And with that, the white cat leapt atop a tall dresser and fell asleep.

A lot of help she was, Spinach chuckled, rolling her eyes. *Sheesh. I guess I'm on my own here!*

In the days that followed, Spinach got to training her body and mind in preparation for whatever mission the future had in store for her, fortified with the knowledge that her armor would give her the power to do incredible things.

Bam! Bam! Bam! She bopped the tetherball, which swung back and forth. It didn't stand a chance against her lightning-fast eye-paw coordination!

"Poopus disappearus," she whispered, and within moments her litter box was scooped and clean as a whistle.

Scratch-scratch-scratch! She sharpened her claws, which shined in the sun like little pointy daggers.

It seemed she was growing more powerful by the day, and yet she wondered to herself what it was all for. If she was meant to take a different pathway, certainly there must be more out there for her than this simple training station! She knew that if she wanted to find her purpose, she would have to break free and explore the rest of Fosterland.

With one paw in front of the other, Spinach dug her claws into the scratching post and lifted herself higher. *Reach, claw, lift. Reach, claw, lift.* Her eyes focused on the ceiling above, she pulled herself closer and closer to the top, until she was towering over the fortress walls, looking out over a wide landscape.

Believe in yourself. You can do anything in your super-suit, she told herself, and held her breath as she made a giant leap of faith.

Whoosh! With aerodynamic ease, she soared over the walls and out into the room.

It felt like a thousand glittering stars were swirling around her tummy. "Watch out, world . . . it's Super Spinach!" she called as her feet sprang forward, launching her around the room like a caffeinated cheetah. Never before had she felt so free!

With unprecedented zoomies, she was galloping and gliding, frolicking and sliding. She ran up the side of a wall and pushed off with her feet, calling out, "I can fly!" But shortly after, she tumbled onto the floor.

Hmm.

Scratching her head, she looked over to a long curtain, and without thought or worry, she hurled herself upward and gripped the loose fabric, climbing higher and higher with her prickly claws digging into the threads. She made it to the tippy-top and balanced with all four paws on the curtain rod.

"I . . . can . . . *fly*!" she called as she jumped all the way from the ceiling and felt the breeze against her silver cheeks.

Suspended in the air, she saw an amazing bird's-eye view of the room. She listed all the things that she could see.

A big fluffy bed.

Two small side tables.

The dresser where my super-sock had been.

A kitten super-station.

Another super-station?

Wait . . . there's another super-station?

She came hurtling toward the ground with one big *thump*, landing on all four paws on a cat bed that was not hers. *What is this place?*

Spinach's eyes widened, and her ears darted to the side as she suddenly heard the sound of tiny paws clapping together.

"That. Was. *Pawesome!*" said a small voice behind her.

Spinach's fur stood on end as she jumped straight into the air and spun 180 degrees. There, in a tiny red hut shaped like a strawberry, she saw a small kitten clapping in adoration. With black-and-white fur, bright blue eyes, and stubby legs, she was rounder than a hedgehog and not one ounce larger.

"Who are you?" Spinach sniffed.

"I'm Chickpea," said the fuzzy roundlet, smiling a gummy pink smile. She was about two-thirds the size of Spinach, with cheeks like a chipmunk and feet like a little mouse. "And you're . . . well, you're amazing! How did you do that giant jump?"

Spinach blushed. "I'm Spinach," she started. "Super Spinach. I guess you could say I'm kind of a hero or something."

Chickpea's face lit up. "A *superhero*?! That's so cool. What kind of powers do you have? Show me!"

Spinach thought for a moment. *Hmm.*

She looked at Chickpea, who was gazing
up at her with big soft eyes.

"Okay, like . . . I can read minds."

"What am I thinking?" Chickpea said,
lifting an eyebrow.

Spinach held her paw to her head and closed her eyes. "You're thinking . . . yes . . . that's it. You're thinking . . .'I'm hungry'!"

Chickpea's jaw dropped. "You really are a mind reader! I could totally go for a warm bottle right now."

Spinach giggled. "I can also run at warp speed. Watch this." She zoomed in a circle around the strawberry hut so fast that Chickpea's eyes couldn't keep up and she fell to the side from the dizziness of trying.

"And I have superstrength and agility," Spinach continued as she jumped high, reached for the top of the super-station wall, and pulled herself to the top. She tiptoed around the edge, balancing her weight back and forth like an acrobat.

"Wow!" Chickpea exclaimed. "You are really something! I wish I could do all that. I can barely walk without flopping over, you know." She clumsily wiggled her way to the center of the fortress, her stubby triangular tail sticking straight up like a go-cart flag, and flopped to the side. With her squishy pink belly exposed and her tiny feet sticking straight out, she flailed around like an upside-down turtle. "A little help?"

Spinach rolled her over and patted her on the head. "You know, not so long ago, I couldn't do any of these things either. But then I got my very own chest armor, and it gave me these supernatural abilities! All my power comes from right here in my super-suit!" She tapped her chest with pride.

"A super-suit? Wow! I've never seen anything like it. You're the coolest, Spinach." She inhaled quickly and covered her mouth. "Eep! Sorry, I meant to call you *Super Spinach*!"

Spinach breathed a deep breath and smiled. She knew all too well what it felt like to look up to other kittens, but never in her life had a kitten looked up to her. Now she had her very own roly-poly protégé, and for the first time ever, she was the leader of the pack.

She hopped into the squishy bed and

slowly sank deep into the sides until she was entirely enveloped in plush. With a muffled voice, she said to Chickpea, "You're pretty cool, too, you know."

Chickpea looked around, but Spinach seemed to have vanished. "Where'd you go?"

"I'm right here," Spinach said, obscured by the fluffy bed.

"Did you go invisible?!" Chickpea squealed.

Spinach closed her eyes and smiled. "Mm-hmm. It's just another one of my special powers, I suppose!"

CHAPTER 5

Sock Collection

Each morning, Spinach's purrsonal assistant kept her looking fresh by combing her fur with a soft toothbrush and giving her a new clean super-sock. It felt a little uncomfortable when she would take off the old super-sock— not because it hurt her physically, but because without it, she just felt so . . . plain. Fortunately, it would only be off for a minute or so during her costume change, and each super-sock was always better than the last.

There was a watermelon sock, a taco sock, and a heart sock. There was a sock with unicorns, a sock with rainbows, and one with little vegetables, too! The socks made her feel special and filled with courage. She collected them all in a small pile under her favorite blanket, and she loved to pull out her super-sock collection and show off the latest fashion to Chickpea.

"Here we have a look complete with sparkly stars," Spinach said as she strutted down the catwalk. "With this sock comes the power of the high jump.

Watch and observe!" She reared back, then jumped so high into the sky that she practically left Earth's orbit! Chickpea watched in amazement as she bounded overhead, her paws touching the stars and gripping the moon.

"Out of this world!" Chickpea exclaimed.

"Next up, we have a jungle sock. With this sock, I can have the power of transformation! Now, close your eyes and count to ten . . . ," she said, silently leaping from the playpen and hiding in a potted plant in the corner.

Chickpea closed her eyes and counted on one paw. "One . . . two . . . three . . . four . . . um, that's all the toe beans I have. I don't know how to count any higher. . . ." She opened her eyes and found that Spinach had vanished. "Spin? Spinny? Spinach? Where'd ya go?"

Spinach tried not to rustle the leaves with her giggles as she hung on to a branch. "Do you see me?"

Chickpea squinted. "I can hear you, but . . . wait, did you transform into a tree?"

Spinach jumped out of the pot and laughed. "Can you be-leaf it? Hahaha! Okay, what's next . . . ?"

She pulled out a sock covered in sequins and smiled. "This one gives me the power of song and dance!"

Somersaulting across the room, she climbed to the top of the bed and stomped on a keyboard until a song began to play.

"Hit it, boys!" she called out as a big band song came on, and she tap-danced across the keys to the jazzy sound of saxophones and trumpets. She grabbed her toothbrush and twirled it over her head like a baton, then sang into the bristles:

**"Oh, I'm a super-kitten
with a super-suit.
My paws are full of magic,
and I'm really cute.
If you see something fluffy
up there in the sky,
it's Super Spinach flying by!"**

She did an amazing spiral dive, landing on the cat bed and dancing without missing a beat. Chickpea nodded along and tapped her paws, trying to keep up with Spinach's dance moves, but she was hardly coordinated at all! Every time she began to really get into the groove, she stumbled around like she had four left paws.

"Take my paws!" Spinach called, and with Chickpea's paws in hers, they danced and danced to the music she had seemingly created from her feet. Spinach spun in a circle with such momentum that Chickpea's little body lifted off the floor, her toes pointed outward as she twirled.

"Whee! I'm flying just like you!" she squealed. "Spin me, spin me!"

In their dizziness, they plopped onto a blanket and laughed.

"Oh, Spinach. You're incredible!" Chickpea squealed, leaning in for a big hug. She tapped on Spinach's chest armor and giggled. "Even if hugging you feels like hugging a big can of tuna!"

Spinach laughed. "Yeah, it's a little clunky, but that's where all my powers come from!"

"You can do so many things I can only dream of," Chickpea said, looking up at the stars and the moon. "If only I could have my own supercool outfit, then I'd be able to join you on adventures and do all the things you can do, too!"

Spinach could understand how Chickpea was feeling. She knew how bad it felt to sit on the sidelines, watching other kittens have all the fun. And so she tugged at the bottom of her sock in deep thought. *Hmm.*

She walked over to her stack of socks and picked up a soft pink one with a heart pattern on it. "Chickpea, this sock

has the power of friendship and adventure. If you ask me, it's not made to be worn by one cat . . . ," she said, digging her teeth into the bottom of the sock and tugging at it until the fabric began to slowly tear. "It's made for two."

Tugging and shredding, she divided the sock into two parts: a belly shirt for her and a skinny band of cloth for Chickpea to wear as a sash.

"Chickpea, I now pronounce you my super-sidekick," she said, placing the fabric around her.

Chickpea smiled big, her little baby teeth starting to emerge. "Just think of all the things we'll be able to do now . . . together!"

CHAPTER 6

Let Me-Owt

The sun rose on another new day in Fosterland, but Chickpea was still snoring away with her super-sash covering her eyes. Spinach paced back and forth, eager for excitement, but her friend was snoozing, and the so-called headmistress was nowhere to be seen! It seemed that if she wanted an adventure to begin, she would have to be the one to make it happen.

"Ahem!" Spinach cleared her throat loudly and bumped Chickpea, who quickly pulled the fabric from her eyes and stood at attention.

"Chickpea, you're my super-sidekick now. And as my super-sidekick, you're going to have to stick by my side and take risks."

"Okay. Like what?" Chickpea asked.

"Like today we're going to find out what lies beyond that door." Spinach gestured toward the bedroom door, which was tall and had a shiny silver handle. "Adventure awaits, and there's no time to waste!"

Spinach jumped over the fortress wall

and called out to Chickpea, who was still yawning, "Are you with me?"

Chickpea looked up at the wall. "I've never climbed anything that tall. I don't know if I can do it."

Spinach pressed her face against the panel and furrowed her brow. "Chickpea, with your super-sash, you can do anything. Believe in its power, and you can get it done!"

Chickpea stretched her arms out in front of her, yawning a massive yawn, then set her eyes on the task ahead. She straightened the sash, wiggled her butt, and jumped with her arms straight up in the air. *Bam!* Her claws caught the top of the wall, and she looked out in amazement. "Holy tuna fish! Look at me! I'm doing it!"

"Go, Chickpea, go! Lift yourself up! There's power in that sock sash!"

Pulling herself up with her little legs, she strained and tugged until at last she tumbled over the edge of the wall and came plummeting down on the other side. "Did you see that?!"

Spinach was the one clapping now. "I told you: you've got powers just like me. Now let's go open that door!"

They zipped over to the door, which was tall and looming. Spinach jumped up and grabbed ahold of the handle, which swung downward. Dangling in the air, she called down to her sidekick, "Push!"

Chickpea pushed and pushed until the door gave way and creaked open. "High four!" Spinach called out as she hopped down and congratulated her friend for achieving such a feat of strength.

They popped their heads around the doorway, peering from side to side. "The coast is clear," Spinach whispered, and they tiptoed down the hall. "Let's find out what this Fosterland place is really all about."

Outside the room, the walls were lined with tall shelves containing stacks of books and tiny shiny trinkets. *What is all this?* Spinach wondered as she pawed at a porcelain cat figurine and knocked it off the shelf.

Thunk!

Chickpea jumped back. "Eep! That startled me! For a second I thought there was another cat here!"

Spinach rolled the statue on its side, and they both sniffed at it. "Nope, just us."

"*Mew!*" squeaked a voice in the distance.

"Did you hear that?" Chickpea whispered.

"It was probably just your tummy rumbling," Spinach said as they continued down the hall.

"*Mew! Mew! Meep!*" The voices multiplied.

Spinach raised an eyebrow and turned to Chickpea. "Did you just sneeze?"

Chickpea shook her head side to side.

"I'm telling you, I can hear something strange. . . ."

They arrived at a large door at the end of the hallway and heard an undeniable high-pitched cry:

"*ME-OW! ME-OW! ME-OW!*"

Chickpea poofed into a perfect sphere of fluff. "Are they saying, 'let me-owt'?"

Spinach arched her back and glared. "I can hear it, too: 'Let me-owt!' Chickpea . . . it sounds like there *are* other cats here . . . and they sound trapped! This is our moment! We've got to *do something*!"

Without a second thought, she called out, "Liquid cat, activate!" and melted into a furry puddle, sliding under the doorway with ease.

Chickpea, left alone in the hallway, looked from side to side and frantically repeated, "Umm . . . liquid cat, activate!" She shoved her head under the door, but her furry rump momentarily jammed as her feet wriggled behind her. "I said: Liquid! Cat! Activate!" she called again, and melted down enough to follow her friend.

Inside, the room was pitch-black. "I don't see anyone!" Spinach called out. "Little kittens, where are you?"

"Mew! Mew!" they responded from somewhere unknown.

Chickpea darted around the perimeter

of the room, feeling the floor with her pink toe beans. Banging about in the dark, she stepped on a little switch, and . . . *click!* "Super-sunbeam!" she called out as the room filled with light.

"Chickpea, you genius!" Spinach tapped her on the head.

With the lights on, they could see now that they were standing in a most peculiar place. They were surrounded by tall shelves containing colorful medicines and bottles of various liquids and powders. "Where *are* we?" Chickpea asked.

Spinach began to tug on a filing-cabinet drawer with all her might. "Help me out, Chicky!" she cried. They strained and pulled until it opened, and inside they found a stack of folders. Within the folders, they found papers containing photos and profiles for five precious little babies.

In the photos, each of the babies was so small that they barely had their eyes open. Three little tabbies and two black kittens were pictured alongside a list of strange scribbles in a language they didn't understand.

"That's them!" Chickpea shrieked. "That's gotta be them!"

Spinach opened folder after folder and flipped through the documents. And as she turned the page . . . she found a strange sheet with a photo of

Chickpea and a sheet with a photo of herself!

She gasped. "*What* in the *world*?"

"Spinach, this is giving me the heebie-jeebies! What is going on here? Why are our pictures here?" Chickpea said as the voices of the kittens grew louder and louder. "Is this some kind of . . . kitten factory?"

"*Mew! Mew! Meep!*" the kittens continued to cry.

"Maybe this place isn't what we thought it was at all . . . ," Spinach worried.

They rummaged through the drawers, slinked through the closet, and dug through tall stacks of blankets. "I don't

see kittens anywhere!" said Spinach, searching high and low. "But I've got an idea. . . ."

She ran to the curtain and dug in her claws. "We have to climb to the top so that we can get a better view. Come with me!" She pulled and tugged her way to the top, and Chickpea followed behind. "Don't look down!"

Up, up, up. They worked their way to the very top of the curtain rod, and Chickpea squealed in shock. "I can't believe I did that!"

"We can do anything, Chickpea!" Spinach responded. "Now, let's find those kittens. . . . Look—over there!"

Atop a table, in a strangely lit box,

five tiny faces were peering out at them, crying. "Mew! Mew! Mew!"

Chickpea gasped. "They're in a *box*! Who on earth would trap kittens inside of a box, and why?"

"No time to ask questions," Spinach said, holding out her paw. "Take my paw. Do you believe in yourself?"

Chickpea bit her lip and placed her shaky paw in her friend's. "I believe in both of us."

With a countdown of "three, two, one," they jumped straight out into the room together, soaring through the air.

"Here comes Super Spinach!"

"And Super Chickpea, too!"

Suspended in air, they both felt

positively invincible and ready to save the day.

"We're coming for you, babies! Chickpea, prepare for landing in three . . . two . . . one!" Their eight paws slammed against the table as they touched down. They'd made it to the top!

Now that they were closer, they could see that these kittens were in no ordinary box. It was some kind of strange warming machine, covered in colorful buttons, and they were stuck inside. Five tiny noses reached over the edge. *Let me-owt!* they seemed to cry.

Spinach extended a paw toward the babies, but just before she reached their faces, her paw hit some kind of invisible wall. *Tap-tap-tap.* She tapped at it with frustration, smooshing her toe beans against the clear partition.

"Holy fish sticks. It's a forcefield!" Chickpea gasped. "Maybe these buttons can deactivate it?"

Beep! Beep-beep! Beep-beep-beep!

Chickpea got to hacking, smacking the buttons with passion.

"Do you actually know what you're doing, Chicky?" Spinach asked.

Chickpea smiled. "Of course I do. I can do anything, remember? For all we know, I'm a technological whiz!" She continued to smack away.

Meanwhile, Spinach noticed that the box was attached to the wall by a long black cable. She tugged at the cable using her superstrength and pulled until it released from the wall and the entire unit shut down.

"Lasso incoming!" she called out, and swung the cable over her head, wrapping it around the handle at the base. "Help me pull!"

They tugged and tugged and tugged . . . and . . .

Crash! They fell to the floor, knocking down vials and tubes along the way.

They'd made quite the ruckus, and with the sound of footsteps quickly approaching, they turned to each other in panic. "Chickpea, turn off the sun!"

Chickpea hopped on the lamp switch, and the room went dark. They stood as still as statues as footsteps entered the room. A giant human plugged the cable back into the wall, pushed several buttons, and slowly walked around.

Chickpea gulped. "Spinach, I'm scared. Is this the bad guy?"

"Shh!" Spinach replied, slinking underneath the table. She listened intently, frightened of being discovered by whatever wicked person was keeping files on all the kittens and keeping babies in a box.

For a moment, the footsteps stopped, and then . . . *Eep!* Two hands picked up Spinach and Chickpea and held them to her face.

Spinach shrieked. "Let us go, you monster! You creep!" She paused in shock. "You . . . *you*?"

It was the purrsonal assistant.

Now they were *really* horrified.

The assistant carried them out of the room with a flabbergasted look on her face, but Spinach and Chickpea were the truly confused ones. They stared at each other in panicked silence.

"We'll be back for you, babies," Spinach whispered as the door closed. "That's a promise. We'll be back."

CHAPTER 7

The Laundry Chute

Now that Spinach and Chickpea knew there were babies out there who needed them, it was all they could talk about.

"Why do you suppose she even *has* them in that weird warm box?" Spinach asked.

"Can you believe the nerve of that lady, undoing all my hacking work with those buttons?" Chickpea grumbled.

"For real! And why does she have files on all the kittens . . . including us? There is something really fishy about all this. . . ."

Chickpea licked her lips. "Fishy?"

"Not like that, Chickpea. I mean that it's creepy."

Chickpea shook her head. "Oh, yeah. Totally."

Spinach was perturbed. Ever since their outing, the giant human had thrown a wrench in all their plans. The doors were now double-locked, and barricades had been placed underneath the doorways to counteract their liquid-cat abilities.

It all made very little sense to Spinach.

Her purrsonal assistant, who had initially seemed to be on her side, now seemed to be putting up roadblocks to prevent her from using her superpowers.

"Maybe I'm getting too powerful," Spinach thought out loud. "Maybe she's threatened by all my abilities. Maybe she's been against us this *whole time!*"

They could hear footsteps in the hall—the purrsonal assistant was about to enter the room. They looked at each other with huge eyes.

"Spinny, what do we do?" Chickpea shrieked.

"Just play it cool. Act like you're not upset. *We can't let her know how much we know,*" Spinach whispered emphatically.

The assistant entered the room and lowered a dish of food for them. Chickpea immediately began to stuff her cheeks, but Spinach only took little licks while she tilted her head to look up at the assistant, who was looking right back at her. *Some nerve, thinking she can placate us with pâté*, Spinach thought. *Like we're just going to forget that she locks babies in boxes!*

She glanced over at Chickpea to exchange looks, but Chickpea was focused fully on staying in character and gobbling up the delicious meal in front of her. She was a great double agent!

After the meal, it was time for the assistant to remove Spinach's sock, as she did every morning. Spinach, pretending things were normal, raised her arms, and the sock was lifted over her head.

But this time, the assistant didn't put another sock on her. With her back turned to them, she walked toward the door.

Spinach looked in her direction. *Why hasn't she given me a new sock? Something seems really peculiar. . . .*

She held a paw to her chest armor. With only half a super-suit, she felt like half a super-cat.

Spinach looked at Chickpea, confused. With her voice low, she muttered, "She didn't give me a sock today. Oh well, that's okay. I'll just pull something from my sock collection. . . ."

She lifted the blanket where she stored her sock collection and found that it was completely, utterly, 100 percent empty.

"Psst. Chickpea. Did you move my socks?"

Chickpea, with her face still covered in gushy wet food, responded by shaking her head. Spinach flung the blankets over her head, getting louder as panic set in. "Seriously, Chickpea, this isn't funny. Where are my super-socks?"

Chickpea licked her face. "Why would I take your socks?"

Spinach swung her head toward the

door and gasped at the sight of crumpled fabric in the assistant's arms. She let out an earth-shattering scream: *"The assistant stole my super-socks!"*

The duo quickly hopped out of the playpen and ran over to the doorway, sneaking through the crack just as it was being closed. The purrsonal assistant, who was busy throwing the socks into a hole in the wall, didn't notice that they had escaped.

"She did *not* just throw my socks into the trash! That evil lady!" Spinach whisper-shouted as Chickpea covered her mouth with her paws.

"Shh! Let's hide!" Chickpea said, dragging Spinach around the corner.

They peeked as the assistant moved down the steps, then the two friends ran to the chute where the socks had been thrown.

"Hop up with me!" Spinach exclaimed. They leapt to the top of the chute, not expecting to suddenly find themselves free-falling through a wormhole. . . .

"Whooa-oooh-ooh-oh!"

They fell and fell, tumbling through a tube in the floor. Or was it the ceiling? It was so disorienting, they hardly had time to think it through before—*thump!* They landed in a giant pile of laundry in the basement.

"Whoa. Did we just teleport?" Spinach said.

She listed in her head the things she could see.

Giant T-shirts.

Crinkled pajamas.

Dirty underpants?!

Chickpea looking back at me, stunned, from underneath a bucket hat.

She threw clothes all about, searching for her super-socks.

"I found one!" she called out, and threw it over her head inside out as quickly as possible.

But before she could look for more socks, the assistant walked down the steps. Chickpea hid underneath the hat, and Spinach did a pencil dive into the laundry basket to obscure herself,

whispering, "Invisibility power, activate!"

The assistant began pushing buttons on a large machine, which started to fill with sudsy water. Suddenly, the basket was being lifted, and Spinach and Chickpea realized that they were moments away from being tossed into the washing machine with all the dirty clothes! Just as they felt the basket tilting, the two kittens shot straight out and bounced off the assistant's head.

"Run!" Chickpea called out as she scooted up the stairs. Spinach straightened her super-suit as she ran close behind her friend.

Frantic, they looked for the quickest place to hide and jumped into the hallway closet. "Shape-shift into a shoe!" Spinach yelled, and each of them jumped into a tall boot.

Thump. Thump. Thump. The footsteps were getting louder as the assistant reached the top of the stairs, calling out for the kittens in her gibberish language.

"Spinach, I'm scared," Chickpea whispered.

"Just stay very . . . very . . . still," Spinach whispered back.

Spinach and Chickpea were squeezed inside the boots, hidden away—except for their little ears, which poked out from the top. For a moment, their powers seemed to be working, because the assistant had ceased her pursuit and moved on to the next distraction: a strange bell at the front door.

Ding-dong.

Through the door, they could hear muffled voices saying hello. The next thing the kittens knew, the closet door swung open for the guest to put away her jacket. Spinach looked up in horror as she realized what was being hung above her head: a white coat, just like the ones she had seen before.

The white-coat vet is in cahoots with the assistant?! It didn't make any sense. The vet helped give Spinach her powers, but now she was working with someone who wanted to take them away?

She tried to hold her paws over her face to keep from revealing their hiding spot, but it was too late. She had cried a shrill "eep!" and the assistant and the white-coat lady were looming over the boots, staring straight at them.

"Chickpea, *run!*" Spinach called out.

Chickpea wiggled out from the boot,

but it was too late—the assistant caught her in her grip.

"This is unjust!" Chickpea screamed.

Spinach, who was now in the hands of the vet, yelled and writhed. "This has to be some kind of conspiracy! The white-coat lady and the assistant are working together, Chickpea! This goes deeper than we think! This . . . goes . . . *deep*!"

"This is an outrage! They'll never get away with this!" Chickpea hissed.

Their plan was falling apart. Spinach and Chickpea had been caught escaping, the socks had been seized, and now they were being carried back to their super-station by the two wicked ladies. Chickpea was plopped down on her fluffy bed, but Spinach was placed up on the bedside table, looking over the room.

The assistant removed Spinach's sock again.

"How could you do this?! I trusted you!" Spinach squealed.

This is it, she thought. *They're stripping me of my powers.*

She fussed and wiggled, but her resistance was futile. With one hand, the white-coat lady held Spinach's head in the forward position so that all Spinach could see was the wall ahead. With the other, she pulled out a small pair of scissors and began to gently trim the small sutures around the chest plate. *Snip-snip-snip.*

Spinach felt a weight being lifted from her skin. She breathed a deep breath and held her paw to her chest, only to find that . . .

. . . the chest plate was completely gone.

CHAPTER 8

Powerless

Spinach was inconsolable. Without her chest armor and her super-sock, she felt completely immobilized, like a bird with clipped wings. She backed into the corner of the playpen, cowering and confused, and hung her head in sadness. *I'm back to the way I used to be at the animal shelter. So frail. So weak. So . . . alone.*

"My powers. They're . . . gone," she said.

Chickpea wiped Spinach's tears with her tail. "It's okay, Spinny. I'm here."

"Why would anyone want to be friends with me now? I can't play. I can't adventure. I can't do anything!"

Chickpea was at a loss for words. How do you comfort a friend who has just lost everything? She pulled the sock sash off and said, "Maybe we can share this?"

Spinach sobbed. "Oh, Chicky, you are so sweet, but without my chest armor, I'm completely powerless."

"But what about the babies? We have to help them!"

Spinach cried, "I can't jump over the super-station walls now. I can't open doors or teleport or turn myself invisible. I don't have liquid-cat abilities or superstrength, and I cannot fly. I'm done for, Chickpea. I'm done. I'll never adventure again without my super-powers."

"Maybe we can find you another super-sock. There's got to be a way." Chickpea hopped over the super-station walls and began to climb the dresser drawers. "Where does she keep her socks?"

Spinach sniffled. "Top drawer."

Chickpea grasped the drawer handle

with her paws and kicked off the dresser with her legs until the drawer began to open.

"This is positively filled with socks!" she called, and began tossing them down.

But Spinach looked over the socks, fully intact, and sighed. "Oh, Chicky. Thank you for trying. But these aren't super-socks. These are the kind that mean old lady wears on her *feet*. They smell, and they have no special powers. I'm afraid that's it for me."

Chickpea looked at Spinach through the fortress walls and held up a paw. "What do I do now? Remember the babies, Spinach. They need us!"

Spinach fell to the floor in tears. "You'll have to go on without me, Chickpea. Just leave me here alone."

"But I don't want—"

"*Just go!*" Spinach interrupted, and turned away from her friend.

CHAPTER 9

Solo Mission

What was Chickpea to do? She didn't want to leave Spinach behind, but there were babies who needed to be saved, with or without Super Spinach. She had never ventured outside of the super-station without the leadership of her friend, and now she was on her own. She squeezed her sash tightly, trying to soak in the bravery it possessed.

On the one paw, it felt wrong for a sidekick to go on a solo mission. On the other paw, it felt wrong to not go and save the babies. And so she took a deep breath and headed for the door.

Going on an adventure was infinitely more difficult, and less fun, without her friend. Yet, armed with her super-sash and the strength it provided, she successfully overcame the obstacles in her way. She did a high jump, hung from the handle, and swung the door open to escape to the hallway. She tiptoed down the hall and hid quietly around the corner as the assistant exited the creepy baby room. Just as the door was closing, she zoomed silently at the speed of light, making it inside without a trace.

Chickpea turned on the sun, stretched her arms, and looked straight above at the tall table containing the kitten box. "This is my chance," she whispered to herself.

She scaled the curtain, as she had learned to do before. She made it to the top of the curtain rod and wobbled. It was scarier to try to fly without holding Spinach's paw, but she knew she alone had to handle the task at hand. "Here goes nothing. . . ." She inhaled deeply, leapt into the air, and called out, "Super Chickpea, headed your way!"

She landed on the table, which

startled the little babies awake. "Mew! Mew! Meep!"

Chickpea pressed her face against the forcefield. "I'm going to get you out of there! I promise! Now, if only I could just . . . open . . . this . . . door!" Using all her strength, she trembled as she gripped the bottom of the drawer and pushed as hard as she could to crack it open.

A gust of warm air escaped through the crack as she lifted the door. "Ruuuuu-ugh!" Chickpea hollered as it creaked open.

"Mew! Mew! MEW! MEW! MEW!" The voices of the kittens were now louder than ever, no longer muffled by an invisible barrier.

Chickpea had never heard such an earsplitting sound in all her life! With waves of warmth emanating from the box and thundering meows surrounding her, she felt a strange combination of excitement and panic. She held on to her sash and forged ahead bravely, calling out, "Super Chickpea is here to save you! Grab hold of my paw!"

She hopped inside the warm box and scooped up the smallest of the babies: a tiny tabby girl she had seen in the files. "I've got you!" she reassured the baby as she held her against her hip and stepped out of the box. But in the mayhem of the heat, the screams, and the stress, she lost her footing and began to wobble, baby in arms.

"Whoa-oh-oh-noooo!" Chickpea slipped off the table, gripping the little one tightly to her side, and nearly tumbled to the floor when—*boom!* Her super-sash caught on the side of the box, stopping her fall but leaving her and the baby dangling midair, swaying side to side.

Help me-owt! the baby seemed to shriek as she gripped on to Chickpea.

Hanging from her super-sash, defenseless and terrified with an innocent newborn clinging to her for dear life, Chickpea let out a roaring cry: *"Super Spinach!"*

CHAPTER 10

A Friend in Trouble

While Chickpea was off on her solo mission, Spinach had curled into a ball and softly cried herself to sleep. She was certain that her heroic days were over and that she would never know friendship or adventure again. And so she lay in sorrowful slumber, dreaming longingly of the days when she still had her super-suit.

Every time she opened her eyes, she felt her chest and remembered her devastating new reality: she was powerless and alone.

"Super Spinach!" called a voice in the distance. Spinach startled awake and shook her head vigorously, certain she'd heard it in a dream. *Chickpea doesn't need me*, she thought. *No one does.* She curled back up and covered her face with her paws.

"Super Spinach!" the voice called again. This time Spinach sat up and looked toward the door curiously.

"*Super Spinach!*" the voice screamed. It was Chickpea—and it was not a dream. This was real life!

"Chickpea? Chickpea!" Spinach could tell that her friend was in trouble. She looked around the room for someone who could help. In the light of the window, she saw a sleeping silhouette: the white cat.

"Wake up! Wake up!" she called at Eloise.

Eloise slowly turned toward Spinach, opening her one yellow eye and gazing in silence.

"My friend is in trouble!" Spinach expressed in panic. "Can you do something? Can you go help her?"

Eloise turned toward the window. "I am too large to fit under a door, and besides . . . it's sunshine hour. This seems more like a job for you, Super Spinach."

Spinach shook her head. "Can't you see I'm no superhero at all? I can't save her! I can't do *anything*!" Spinach's heart was thumping in her chest. She felt small and defenseless, like back at the shelter when she couldn't play with the other kittens or chase a crinkle ball or do anything besides sit and watch life happen around her.

"*Help! Super Spinach! Help!*" Chickpea continued to call from the other room.

"Eloise, what can I do?!" Spinach cried. "I feel so weak! You're the head-mistress of this place—can't you give me any guidance at all?"

Eloise turned to her and repeated the

words she'd said on Spinach's first day in Fosterland: "Remember, strength and bravery come only from right here."

"But my armor is gone! My super-sock—vanished! I have no powers any-more. None."

Eloise winked her one eye and repeated herself: "Strength and bravery come only from *right here*." She pointed to her chest firmly.

Spinach huffed. "I don't have time for your rhymes! My friend needs help!"

With no one else to turn to, Spinach couldn't think of her limits or the fact that she didn't have superpowers any-more. She could only think of her friend.

Even if Spinach was sure she would fail, she had to try.

So, without hesitation and with a surge of frustrated energy, she jumped over the edge of the super-station, surprising herself. *What in the . . . ?*

"I was trying to tell you . . . ," Eloise began, but Spinach had no time to waste. She cartwheeled across the room, flipped head over heels in the air, and swung the door open with one mighty paw.

Spinach slid down the hallway, faster than lightning and smoother than a seal, until she reached the barricade outside the door.

"Help me, Super Spinach!" Chickpea shrieked from the other side. "This baby and I are hanging by a thread—*and it's about to snap!*"

CHAPTER 11

Mission Accomplished?

With powerful strength, Spinach ripped the barricade from underneath the door, throwing it across the hall with a forceful *slam!* She slid underneath and looked up to see Chickpea dangling in the air, holding tightly on to a tiny tabby. The threads of the supersash were pulling apart, stretching and threatening to snap at any moment!

Spinach let out a rallying cry: *"Super Spinach is here!"*

"Spinach! It's you! *My hero!*" Chickpea called down to her, her little paws suspended overhead.

Spinach rocket-leapt to the top of the table and extended a paw to her sidekick. "Take my paw! Do you believe in me?"

Just as the final thread began to break, Chickpea grabbed ahold of Spinach's paw and said, "I believe in *us*!"

Spinach pulled with all her might, hoisting Chickpea and the baby upward with nothing but the strength of her limbs. "Got you!" Spinach called out as she pulled them onto the table, and the three of them fell into a kitten pile.

The baby lay atop Spinach's chest, which was rising and falling with each heavy breath. "You're safe now, little one," she said, panting and patting the baby on the head. "I've got you. We've got you."

She looked to Chickpea, who was beside her, staring in awe.

"But . . . your super-sock is gone! How did you . . . ?" Chickpea said, confused and amazed.

Spinach sat upright, holding her paw to her chest. *Strength and bravery come only from right here*, she thought, and it suddenly all made sense. "That's it! The power wasn't in our super-suits, Chicky. The power is *in our hearts*!"

Chickpea grasped at what remained of her tattered super-sash. "You mean . . . I don't even need this thing?"

"It sure seems that way," Spinach replied. "But it might come in handy for one last task. . . ."

Spinach ripped the cable from the wall once more. Using the remaining scraps from the super-sash, she secured the cord to the circular bed where the kittens lay using a firm triple knot. "We've got babies to save! Hop inside and keep those babies safe," she said as they all loaded into the bed like passengers in a lifeboat. "Lowering in three, two, one . . ." She helped them down to the floor slowly and gently using the long cable, then hopped down gracefully to join them.

"Spinach, we did it!" Chickpea had tears in her eyes. She gave Spinach a giant hug, their little furry chests squeezed tight against one another, with two hearts pounding in sync. "We had power inside us the whole time!"

"And I guess I'm a better hugger now, too, eh?" Spinach said, tapping her furry chest.

They were beaming with joy and accomplishment, amazed by the bravery of their adventurous feat, when suddenly one of the little kittens tugged on Chickpea's side and said:

"Um, excuse me? I'm cold!"

The others chimed in: "Mew! Mew! We're cold, too! Put us back in the box! Mew!"

Chickpea looked down at the baby, then looked at Spinach, stunned. "But . . . we saved you."

"Saved us from what? Our warm and cozy bed? From all the soft blankets the nice lady gives us?"

"Nice lady?" Spinach's face twisted as she looked to Chickpea for a reaction.

"Why were you always screaming and crying if you didn't want to escape, then?" Chickpea grunted.

"Um, because we're babies! Duh! Mew! Mew!"

Spinach scratched her head. *The babies actually like it in that warm box? Huh. That must mean . . . that the evil lady might not be so evil after all. . . .*

Just then, the purrsonal assistant walked into the room holding a tray with a fresh bottle of formula.

"Oh my gosh. Chickpea . . . I think we've made a terrible mistake." Spinach covered her face with her paws. "I am so embarrassed."

The purrsonal assistant reached down and picked up all the kittens in their bed, and seemed to giggle. Spinach tried her telepathic messaging to see if she still had the power to communicate with her.

Purrsonal assistant, I think we have made a bit of an error. Please return all of us to our comfortable headquarters and prepare us a meal of our preference—a bottle for the little ones and, if you don't mind, a nice celebratory pâté for myself and my sidekick, Chickpea.

Whether or not it was heard, her request was met. As the little kittens were placed back inside the box, they purred and purred. "Thank mew!" they said. "Yay, it's so toasty and warm!" They watched as the purrsonal assistant fed the babies one after another, their little ears wiggling back and forth. And they realized that the purrsonal assistant, in fact, wasn't a bad guy at all.

"Well, this is awkward!" Spinach laughed.

The assistant walked them back to their super-station, where they talked about everything that had happened over a can of moist cat food.

"Let me get this straight," Chickpea

said. "Those babies didn't need to be saved." Spinach nodded. "And you don't need your armor." Spinach nodded again. "And I don't need my super-sash." Spinach nodded a final time. Chickpea sat very still, aside from her stuffed cheeks, and chewed in contemplative silence. "But we're still superheroes, right?"

"Chicky, I think you and I can be anything we want to be."

CHAPTER 12

New Neighbors

A week had passed, and Spinach and Chickpea were yawning and waking up in their super-station. Spinach's ears perked up at the sound of footsteps in the hall, and she nudged Chickpea to say, "I predict that our breakfast will arrive in three . . . two . . . one!" The door opened, and like magic, there was the assistant, holding two dishes of food.

"I must say, I've always admired your keen ability to see the future, Super Spinach!" Chickpea winked, licking her chops in anticipation of their meal. Although they'd both grown to realize that their amazing abilities were simply part of their spectacular growth and bravery, they had a good sense of humor about their status as would-be superheroes.

"Foodus disappearus!" Chickpea squealed before gobbling up her entire meal in four swift bites.

What came next was something that neither of them could predict. The purrsonal assistant began to click together tall plastic panels, creating another fortress adjacent to theirs and filling it with blankets and beds. *Are we getting neighbors?* Spinach wondered.

The next thing they knew, a basket of kittens was being escorted into the room, and as it lowered into the adjacent pen, they could see that it was the five kittens from the box . . . only now they looked much bigger!

"Hey there, new neighbors!" Chickpea waved.

The kittens looked at one another and smirked. "Oh great, it's our *heroes*," the tiniest tabby muttered sarcastically, making the others crack up. "What kind of mission are you going on next? Saving us from the spooky, scary bottle?"

Spinach and Chickpea laughed along
with the babies, aware that they'd gotten
a *little carried away* with their so-called
rescue mission.

"Good one," said Spinach. "I guess

you're right: superheroes don't exist!"
She paused and smiled a tiny smile.
"Except . . . if I'm not a superhero . . .
why is it that I can read your minds?"

The kittens tilted their heads with
curiosity.

"You can't read minds!" snickered a
black kitten.

Spinach giggled. "Oh, you're probably right. Anyhow, I'll just be on my
merry way. . . ."

She turned as if she was about to
leave, when the kitten called out,
"Prove it!"

Spinach held her paw to her head
and pretended to be deep in thought.

"Hmm. My powers tell me that . . . yes, yes, that's it . . . you're hungry!"

All five kittens sat straight up in total shock. They whispered to one another in amazement, "How did she do that?!"

CHAPTER 13

Super Sisters

"Bam!" Chickpea called out as she batted at a crinkle ball, which flew across the room.

Spinach ran like a gazelle, flying into the air and catching the ball between her paws. "Whoo! Got it. Right back at ya!" She hit the ball back toward her friend. "Pow!"

On the other side of their clear glass

panels, five little heads bobbled up and down, watching them with focus and admiration. The tiny kittens, who had introduced themselves as Welly, Nelly, Darwin, Logan, and Alice, were just reaching the age where they were start-ing to want to play, and the sight of the crinkle ball was positively mesmerizing.

"They're so cool," muttered Welly to Nelly. "I wish I could do that."

Spinach pounced, then looked toward the playpen to see that all eyes were fixed on her. In that moment, it struck her that those little kittens were much like she once was: stuck behind a barrier, watching older kittens have all the fun.

"Believe it or not, you can do anything you put your mind to!" Spinach said with a smile, and tossed the ball into their playpen. "Here—you try!"

The kittens gathered around the crinkle ball, their eyes bigger than saucers, nervous to touch it for the very first time. They sniffed around the edge of the toy, and when the tiniest tabby, Alice, accidentally tapped it with her nose, it made a rattling sound that made them all jump back in surprise. "I can't!" she squeaked, and hid behind her brothers.

The biggest brother, Logan, whose fur was all poofed out, agreed. "I don't know if we can do it. Besides, you guys are heroes . . . and we're just babies!" At his side, Darwin sat nodding his head.

"I used to feel the same way, but hear me out: when you believe in yourself, you have the power to do a lot more than you think," Spinach said. "Go ahead and give it a shot."

Logan took a deep breath. He lifted the crinkle ball with his claws, and with the flap of his wrist, it went flying into the air. Without a thought, Alice and Darwin jumped for it, and both clamped down with their tiny paws.

"Whoa!" they both said in unison.

The game was a hit! As the babies

played for the very first time, Spinach and Chickpea watched from outside the pen, coaching them.

"Go babies!" Chickpea hollered.

"Be strong, little ones! You've got all the bravery you need right here,"

Spinach called as she touched her heart.

Chickpea looked up at Spinach with adoration. "You know, Spinny, I still think you're a superhero. You're so loving and kind. I hope you know that you really are a hero to those little ones—and to me, too!"

Spinach smiled. "I used to think you couldn't be a hero unless you wore some fancy costume, but now I realize how silly I was." She paused, reflecting on her journey. *Even when I was at the shelter, I still had the same big heart,* she thought. "Heroes aren't built from cloth and string. They're built from bravery, and from love. And, Chicky, after all we've been through together, I've sure got a lot of love for you!"

Just then, the door to the room creaked open, and in walked the assistant, with Eloise at her feet. Eloise rubbed against the assistant's leg, looked to the super-duo, and closed her eye.

"Is that a wink or a blink?" Spinach asked.

"It's a wink," Eloise said. "Congratulations, you two. As your headmistress, it brings me great pleasure to tell you that it looks like your mission is complete."

The purrsonal assistant placed something on the bed, and Spinach and Chickpea hopped up to investigate.

"It's a folder," Chickpea said. "Open it."

The five little kittens looked up at them with curiosity. "What is it?"

Spinach grasped the folder and opened it slowly. Inside was the file they'd seen in the baby room—the one with pictures of them. Spinach's and Chickpea's profiles were bound at the top, secured together with a shiny metal clip. And clipped to the papers was something that made her gasp.

"Chicky . . . it's a blue card!"

"A blue card?" Chickpea tilted her head. "What does that mean?"

"It means . . . it means we get to go to Foreverland! We're getting adopted. We did it! We did it, Chicky!"

Chickpea rustled through the papers. "Foreverland? Both of us? Together?"

"Together forever," Spinach said

as she wrapped her arms around her sidekick.

She wiped a happy tear from her eye as she remembered how desperately she had longed for a blue card at the animal shelter and how much she had feared that she might never receive one. But now all the twists and turns in the road made perfect sense because they had led her here. Her blue card wasn't late at all! In this magical moment, her blue card had come right on time.

She took a deep breath, turned to her friend, and said, "Super sisters stick together for life."

Their mission was complete. Chest

to bare chest, they hugged each other tight as the five little kittens cheered in celebration of Spinach and Chickpea: two ordinary cats, yet extraordinary all the same.

The True Story of Spinach and Chickpea

Spinach was only three weeks old when she was found outside without a mama and brought to the San Diego animal shelter. The shelter staff quickly realized that she had been born with a medical condition called pectus excavatum, which occurs when the rib cage is misshapen. They called my nonprofit, Orphan Kitten Club, to see if we could help her, and we said yes! We took her straight from the shelter to the veterinary hospital, where she had chest surgery to create more space for her lungs and heart.

After surgery, Spinach needed to wear a hard chest plate for four weeks while she recovered. Every few days I would cut up a new sock and place it over her chest like a sweater to protect her chest plate. Even though she had just had surgery, and was dressed in a silly sock, she was so incredibly brave and active! She approached life with a can-do attitude and was so excited to feel healthy enough to play. But nothing made her happier than when another little kitten, Chickpea, showed up!

Chickpea was found outside and brought to the shelter when she was just two weeks old. When she arrived in my care, she was a bit smaller than Spinach, but oh so cute and round! After a quarantine period, I opened Chickpea's playpen and let them meet each other for the first time. Chickpea was always fascinated by Spinach, who was a bit older and more coordinated than she was. Together they worked up the bravery to tackle new things like climbing the bed, playing with wand toys, and even breaking out of the bedroom to explore the rest of the house.

Eventually, it was time for Spinach's chest plate to come off, revealing a healthy chest beneath. She had healed beautifully and was ready to get adopted! It was obvious that Spinach and Chickpea were best friends, so it only made sense to find them a forever home where they could stay together forever. Spinach and Chickpea were adopted by a loving couple in San Diego, and they are still having adventures together to this day!

Looking for another great book?
Find it
IN THE MIDDLE.

Fun, fantastic books for kids
in the in-beTWEEN age.

IntheMiddleBooks.com

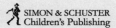

READ & LEARN

with
simon kids

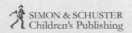